Edition BAES

www.edition-baes.com

Übersetzung: Isabelle Esser
Cover: Peter Feller
Layout: Alexander Augustin · buechermacher.at

Herstellung: Books on Demand GmbH, Norderstedt

ISBN 978-3-9503811-6-0

Elias Schneitter

Austria.Karl

Edition BAES

1

You can't be expected to put up with everything life throws at you.

I mean, where would that get us?

There's only so much you can take.

Those paper pushers in the admin office looked like proper Charlies.

They should know better than to mess with Judge Georgie.

No-one messes with Judge Georgie, the traveling salesman, even if I am retired, a decommissioned traveling salesman, so to speak.

As a rule, I'm as gentle as a lamb, it's just when injustice rears its ugly head that people see my darker side.

And believe me, I don't care if it's the Emperor of China sitting in front of me.

I don't give a hoot because justice is justice.

And I've lived by this principle all my life.

I could've said to myself, what do I care about my wife's decrepit aunt?

After all, she's just another bed-ridden wrinkly.

She's not even right in the head anymore.

She's completely lost her marbles.

You should hear some of the stories she comes out with.

It's almost tragic.

But that's not the point.
Her health insurance refused to pay for her incontinence pads and diapers, even though she keeps wetting the bed because she's incontinent.
Imagine that! I just could not believe it!
They didn't want to pay for the diapers of an old sick woman because it was no longer their remit, they said.
It's things like that that make my blood boil.
I can't help myself.
I kicked that stupid little krank's ass, you know, the one in the office.
Now, auntie gets her incontinence pads and diapers for free again.
She could have afforded to pay for them herself, of course.
She's not exactly poor.
In fact, my eyes nearly popped out my head when I saw her savings.
Her husband had a successful business, you see.
When it was sold, after he'd popped his clogs, she earned some big bucks...
The business was sold abroad, to Germany...
Anyway, as I was saying, I could've told myself not to bother with my wife's aunt.
But things like that just get to me...
I mean, we all know what it's like with these bureaucrats.

I could write volumes about it.
And when I think of all the hassle I had when I retired.
It doesn't bear thinking about, because when I do start thinking about it, well...
Georgie, switch off dear, says my wife, when I get too hot under the collar.

There's no point in getting flustered, it will only affect your health.
And it won't change anything anyway, she says.
But that's easier said than done, especially when you've always lived your life by the book and then you see them squandering it all and running everything into the ground.
I want to enjoy my retirement.
Even though I've had some great times over the years, surely that can't have been it?
So that's why I tell myself to remain calm and keep my feet planted firmly on the ground.
Even though that's easier said than done.
I just have to start thinking of those diapers.

2

Now that I'm a pensioner, time doesn't seem to tick by any more slowly.

Not with me anyway.

I've got plenty to do, more than plenty.

It's not for nothing that they say that pensioners are always busy.

I suppose in that sense, I never really retired in the way that people normally do.

But then again, many can't cope with retirement.

Simply because they feel superfluous.

That's why so many die of heart attacks within the first year because they simply don't know what else to do.

Well, I can't say that's been true of me in the past two years.

But then, I didn't really retire properly.

I still give my old boss a hand every now and then.

And then, of course, there's plenty of work to do in the house and garden.

There's always something in need of repair, always work to do in the vegetable patch.

The vegetable patch is my hobby.

But what I can't stand are those slugs gobbling up my lettuce.

I collected a whole pail full of them yesterday and threw them in the canal.

When I got back from vacation – what's a vacation to a pensioner? - you should've seen the state the garden was in – all because of those slimy critters.
But what can you do?
I'm still going on vacation.
Those slugs aren't going to stop me.
We go every year – a whole group of us.
This time round, we were away for three weeks.
Otherwise, it wouldn't have been worth the money.
Burma, Bangkok, Thailand.
Really beautiful places.
It's really worth seeing.
But you should see the squalor.
Living where we do, it's difficult to imagine.
My buddy, Karl, says misery like that can only be eradicated with tough measures.
Politically speaking.
That's the only way to deal with it, he says.
Radical measures from above.
We don't know how good we've got it here in Austria compared to them down there.
The filth, the squalor, the poverty, it's overwhelming…
The country itself is beautiful, well what we saw of it anyway, despite the heat, but the cities, oh God, the cities…
The chicks, though, they were hot.
Especially for that price.

The best thing is, there's no arguments – not like at home with the wife – because thankfully you can't understand a word they say.

Once I took my escort to a hotel and outside there was this kid, with no arms, he was a complete cripple.

Well, I gave him the equivalent of twenty euros. He thanked me, then snatched at the banknote with his mouth because he had no hands.

That's poverty for you.

Our hobos are millionaires by comparison.

I felt so sorry for him that I shoved another twenty euro note in his mouth.

I didn't say a word.

There are no words for things like that.

I've seen so much in my time because I've traveled around a fair bit.

But I've never seen anyone pick up money with his mouth – that was definitely a first.

These people are so friendly and they're so grateful even for the smallest of gifts.

We were generous.

Everything's dirt cheap there anyway.

The whole family lives off the money those hot little chicks earn.

So in a sense, I suppose you could call us aid workers.

Even when we fuck.

They do anything, they get straight to it.

The whole family survives on the takings.

So, as you can imagine, they're highly motivated.
So we really went to town, I tell you.
I won't be bothering my wife for a while, that's for sure.
After all, I'm not twenty anymore.
And three weeks was a bit long.
And it's not the same as it used to be.
I think I'll go on my own next time.
Or maybe with Karl.
You're more independent then and you don't have to worry about anyone else.
Yeah, I think that would be wise.

3

I went to the soccer ground with Karl yesterday.
It was crap.
Back in the day, we used to go there all the time.
These days, only Negroes and good-for-nothing Slavs play because our lot are too lazy to run around.
They're all idle time-wasters.
These days, everyone wants to be a CEO, but they don't want to work for it.
The same is true of soccer.
Big money for no effort, that's what they want.
But these Negroes and Slav wasters are no better.
What I saw yesterday had nothing to do with soccer – absolutely nothing.
But that's hardly surprising as they don't even speak the same lingo.
How are you supposed understand a Negro or an Albanian shepherd.
You just can't.
All they want is our nationality and as soon as they've got it, they sit back and do nothing.
But it's our fault for going to the match.
Afterwards, we went for a beer.
Karl's going to retire soon as well.
Another month, then he's hanging up his boots.
He's as excited about retiring as a little kid before his birthday.

I'll be happy as Larry not to see those assholes anymore, he said.
He's alright, Karl is.
We've got a great surprise up our sleeves for him when he retires.
Us guys have clubbed together and are having a Thai woman flown in for him.
We just have to make sure his wife doesn't get wind of it.
Women are a bit strange that way.
We've got everything arranged.
Karl won't believe his luck.
But we think he deserves it.
We'll put the Thai woman up somewhere else and we'll tell our wives we're going walking for a week.
That way, I'll get something out of it as well.
Karl's retirement went through alright.
Even though he's retiring early.
He's only fifty four so he's got plenty ahead of him.
Yeah OK, he's a civil servant, but still.
He was off sick for a year, well actually, he just stayed at home and they urged him to take early retirement.
Well, I'm up for that alright, were his very words and I don't blame him.
Karl deserves it, he's a great guy.
I'd do the same, if I were in his shoes.
When I retired, God! what a mess that was.

The grief they gave me – you wouldn't believe it, if I told you.

If I hadn't known exactly how things are done in these places, they would never have released me.

And to think it was me who showed them the ropes.

Even though my health was rockbottom.

I was in such a state with my back that I couldn't even crawl out of bed.

Therapies and massages were no help at all.

Except for the ones in Thailand but the bastards don't pay for them, do they.

Well, there was no way I could go back to work.

So what did they do? They tried to screw me over with my pension, even though I'd worked by butt off, never taking a day off sick, but these paper pushers don't give a damn about that.

I'd put in almost forty years of service because we started working at fourteen, not like these days where kids study till they're thirty and cause trouble whilst sponging off the state.

In our day, it was a totally different ball game.

And I pretty much taught those people how to walk.

It's the politicians and crap civil servants of all people who waste millions and then deny the little man on the street – the little man being me – what's rightfully his.

But that's the way they do things in Austria these days.

That's what I said to Karl.

Twice, I had to take my case to the labor court – yes, twice, before getting what was rightfully mine.

I said to Karl back then, I said if Georgie wants to retire, then retire he will.

And that's exactly what I did.

Some days, I couldn't even stand up straight, that's how painful my back was.

I can't abide that word lumbago any more.

This top physician wanted to prescribe me a break at a spa resort but what good would that do?

If my body's in pieces after forty long years of hard slog, I certainly don't want to go to a spa.

I want retirement, that's what I want.

I'm not one of those spongers who go on a four-week break every year and have it paid for by Joe Public.

If it were down to me, I'd abolish these spa trips in the blink of an eye.

Most people only go there to have a fling anyway.

That's the only reason they have these spa treatments.

It makes me think of the stories Karl used to tell me about his colleagues going off to the best spa resorts and being treated like royalty every year.

But it's no use thinking about it.

I only just made it to the end of my stint and then they mistreat me like that, even though I had paid my way all my life.

But that's Austria for you.

The hard workers are always the losers, just like me.
I don't want any favors but I certainly want what I'm entitled to.
Once, when I went to the pension office, I overhead one of those paper-pushing pricks mumbling to one of his colleagues: Look, here comes old lumbago.
To think it was me who showed them the ropes.
I demanded an apology from the top.
And I got one too.
And if I hadn't got an apology, I'd have gone to the press.
The press laps up stories like that.
Karl was right all along – he said, he didn't know what their problem was because you can't prove lumbago, can you!
It's like having a headache.
If I say I've got lumbago, the doctors can stare holes into the x-rays but they'll never find it.
I'm the perfect example of that.
Down at the pension office, no-one ever called me lumbago after that.
They kept their mouths tightly shut and gave me my pension.
If they hadn't given me my pension, they'd have had it coming.
I swore to them they'd get it.
These civil servants, who live off my taxes, tried to tell me whether I have lumbago or not.

I don't want to think about it.
Luckily, I'm the kind of guy who can stand up for himself.
If you can't do that, then you'll always be a loser in this country.
Anyway, I got my retirement when I wanted it.
They can't tell me what to do, not me, Judge Georgie.
But there's no sense in wasting another second thinking about my pension.
I've been retired for two years now.
So what's the point in getting uptight about it now.
I should be thankful – touch wood – that I'm still in pretty good health.
I still have days though where I can't stand up straight.
But Thank God that doesn't happen as often as it used to.

4

I often think you know: What would I do without my garden!
When I feel really low, the garden's the best distraction in the world.
In spite of those god-damn slugs.
Karl always laughs about it.
He says everyone has his poison – some go and watch the game, others drown themselves in drink, some dash like madmen up hill and down dale and you, you get excited over your cabbages.
That's until my nosy neighbor pops his head over the fence and asks: Are the slugs eating everything again?
To think of all the tricks I've used to get rid of this slimy slug invasion.
But you know, these slugs have only been around for a relatively short while.
We didn't have them years ago.
They come over from Russia or somewhere round there.
A pure import.
It's a complete and utter sabotage of our gardens.
By them, the Russian mafia.
They'll be laughing in their sleeves by now.
No doubt, there's a method, a scheme behind it all.
They can't be trusted, them from over there.

I've heard of this Indian species of duck that would be all over the slugs in minutes, but they don't half make a mess.

Besides which, who knows how many Indians I'd need because they can't eat just slugs.

Not in those quantities anyway.

And then if we did have those Indian things in our garden who knows where it would lead.

When it comes to Indians you can't be sure of anything because they just don't fit in.

So after the Russians, we'd be putting up with the Indians from India.

For a while, I sprinkled salt all over them.

They shriveled up alright but the trouble was, I'd have needed my own private salt mine to annihilate them every day.

What I'd like to know is where they all come from.

They must reproduce like turbo-rabbits.

The problem is they have no natural predators to keep them in check.

I also went through a phase where I impaled them all on an iron rod and cut them in two with my secateurs.

It wasn't pleasant to say the least, especially with all that slime squirting out left, right and center.

Once, I even mounted a sharp wedge on the bottom of an old hiking boot and slaughtered them that way.

But that didn't really work very well because they're sticky and so I had trouble shaking them off the sole of my boot.

Now I pick them up with my BBQ tongs every day and toss them by the sack-load into the canal.

You've got to keep at it.

Otherwise it's a losing battle.

Karl once said to me, you know what, someone needs to invent something for that.

You could earn big bucks if you invented something like that.

If you invented something, you could become a millionaire.

I think all the slugs in Austria should be collected and sent back to the Russian mafia.

Back to where they came from.

Then THEY would have to deal with all the rubbish they've dumped on us.

5

There was a time when my wife would tell me off
for comparing this foreign vermin to the slugs in my
garden...
Today though, she's come round to my way of thinking...
I did warn her right at the start, I warned her that
she shouldn't even entertain the thought, because I
knew exactly what would happen.
But my wife would always attack me when I said the
Kebab Munchers were invading our country like the
Russian slime that was taking over my garden.
Everyone needs people around them, my wife would
say.
But not filth like that, I'd reply...
Anyway, I didn't really want to get involved because
her auntie has nothing to do with me and so I don't
care whether Kebab Munchers live in the same place
as her. What's it to me.
Even Karl said he didn't understand my wife.
But what am I supposed to do, after all, she's a
grown woman.
I certainly wouldn't let any of those mafia wise guys
into my home.
They're human beings too, my wife insisted.
They were driven from their homes by war, we have
to help them.

And anyway, their rooms are in the cellar and they have a separate entrance.

But then she realized all right, then she saw what happened.

It's not as though I didn't tell her.

They had parties in the garden, with music blaring out while their kids terrorized the neighborhood…

None of them lifted a finger by going to work.

They all sponge off the state.

Child-care allowance.

But we've got it to spare, haven't we. Pah.

They should never have let the Russians set foot in our country.

I mean, what have they got to do with us?

Let them shoot at each other if that's what they want, but that's their problem not ours!

All we want is a little peace and quiet.

Being nice doesn't get you anywhere in life.

I know what I'm talking about.

I've seen it all.

My wife was being a bit simple there.

But thankfully she's wised up now.

She's seen where it leads.

She gives them a home, a roof over their heads, and how do they thank her? With a police complaint.

We've got to the point in Austria where they get all sorts of state support.

But it's hardly surprising when you look at our government, it's full of Kebab Munchers.

Austrians count for nothing in this country anymore.

If things carry on the way they are, we Austrians will end up being the foreigners in our own country.

I told my wife it's not worth it for the sake of a few shillings.

In Austria, you've got to tread carefully, as the press lap up stories like ours, mutating you into an exploiter when all you were doing was trying to help.

I've even had nightmares about the headlines.

Exorbitant rents for cellar rooms!!! Etc.

Our press gurus don't care much for the truth.

All they're interested in is headlines, sensations and filth.

They're all manipulated.

We all know who's behind it.

The capital all comes from abroad.

And it doesn't take much guessing to know what that means.

The truth doesn't interest anyone.

But what's the point in getting worked up about it.

Karl's quip is right by the way.

He always says that the comparative and superlative of truth is: Truth – lie – press.

He's hit the nail on the head there.

I blame the police complaint against my wife on the relatives.

Especially, the prodigious stepson.
Yes, another fine specimen of a loser that should be swept out of the country with the Russians.
He's never made an effort with his step mother.
A sprog from the first marriage of my wife's uncle.
If it wasn't for my wife, her aunt wouldn't receive any help for weeks on end.
When he does appear out of the blue, all he wants is money.
In the past, when she was still healthy, she would often throw him out.
Sometimes he'd even steal from her.
He was a real waste of space, a good-for-nothing.
As long as I can remember, he's never had a steady job.
He's even been in jail a few times.
He has a few kids dotted about the country, but probably doesn't support them.
He's the perfect example of what happens to a kid whose parents want too much of the best for him.
He always got everything he wanted.
Money was never an issue.
And that was his downfall.
This guy believed his life would always be like that.
My wife would throw him out when he visited her aunt just to sponge off her.
You couldn't trust him as far as you could spit.
He even pocketed his uncle's gold watch.

Well, it certainly wasn't there after he'd left.
That's why my wife hid the savings away from him.
At least, they're safe here, away from that lay-about's prying eyes.
If he'd got his grubby little hands on them, he'd have spent all the money in minutes.
He's a champion when it comes to blowing cash.
Once he squandered tens of thousands in a single night.
As soon as he's got a dime to spare, he invites everyone out.
Then he pays for round after round because he wants to be the centre of attention.
He would've wasted the dough from the company sale in a blink of an eye.
At least, his share of it.
But it's no wonder I suppose, it's easy to waste what you haven't worked hard for.
As far as I know, I think he's on welfare now.
But you can't buy many rounds on welfare.
You can go out for three and then you're skint again.
What a cheek it is that people like that are entitled to welfare.
If it were up to me …
Why can't a man like that get a job?
Just because he thinks it's beneath him, the state has to foot the bill.
All I can say is "Good night Austria".

I don't know what to say.
I mean the money's got to come from somewhere.
And of course, it comes from us because stupid idiots like me worked hard to pay for it all.
And then what happens? We get punished for it.
When I think that I clocked up forty years of hard work, I reckon I must be some kind of klutz.
Our railway workers retire in their early fifties, sit back and laugh at everyone else.
They only worked there so they could rest and still have enough energy for their cowboy jobs on the side.
So don't come talking to me about my retirement.
I've done my share.
It sickens me to think of all the money that's smuggled abroad, such as swindled child support and whatever else there is.
When I look at that aunt's boot neck of a boy who's never done an honest day's work in his life and enjoys all the support that's out there: exemptions, free telephone, free TV, even a free room courtesy of the state.
It makes me sick.
And yet, this kid was given every opportunity imaginable.
Opportunities, that most would bend over backwards to receive.
We had to work hard for everything we got.

Some people think that's beneath them.
And there seem to be more and more of them every day.
Anyone who goes looking for a job in Austria will find one.
You mustn't think you're too precious to work, that's all.
Of course, not everyone's cut out to be a CEO.
But there's nothing wrong with working in a hotel.
Even if you're just washing dishes.
That's still better than nothing.
But we Austrians don't want to.
We think we're above that sort of thing.
And that's why there are so many Russians in our country.
But they only wash dishes until they're entitled to unemployment benefit and as soon as that time comes they don't lift a finger anymore.
And then, they bring the rest of their family over.
If things carry on the way they are, it won't be long before we don't have any say anyway.
It will be the others who have it.
That's already the way it is in Vienna.
Just look at the government.
It's full of foreign names.
The Viennese defended themselves against three sieges by the Turks.
And then during the fourth, they go and cave in.

Just go to the Naschmarkt and see what's going on there.
You won't find anything like it, not even in Istanbul.
That's how extreme it is.
Something has to be done about it.
Someone's got to come down hard on them.
By them, I mean the Russians and the welfare scroungers.
It can't go on like this.
Something should've been done years ago.
Especially those unemployed spongers who take the welfare payments, work quietly on the side and pocket the cash.
I just have to look around me.
It's all plain to see.
You can't fool me.
But then, what incentives are there for unemployed people to look for work.
As things stand, they'd be stupid to get a job, yes stupid.
And this is where the state needs to clamp down.
What can I, the man on the street, do about it?
Karl says he'd give them what-for.
He'd cart all the welfare fraudsters and scum off to a work camp.
I mean what else can you do with hobos like that?
A quick trip to the train station and you've seen it all, I tell you.
I mean you're not doing these people any favors.

At least at a work camp more time would be invested in those losers.

If anything, they'd get used to working again and could be reintroduced to society.

As things stand at the moment, they'll be receiving state handouts till the end of their days.

We can't afford it all in the long run.

Who's going to foot the bill?

Even my dad used to say that Adolf may have made mistakes along the way but where there's light, there's shadow.

If it wasn't for Adolf, we wouldn't be as well off as we are today, my dad always used to say.

And he was right.

My dad never spoke much about the war.

He was a quiet kind of guy.

On the odd occasion he'd say they're taking the easy way out by heaping all the blame on Adolf.

You've got to look at the circumstances close up.

Adolf was a kind of force of nature who descended upon the country.

There's nothing you can do about that.

The Resistance stories always made my dad laugh.

When they pin you against the wall, your resistance evaporates, my dad always used to say.

The people who talk of Resistance today would have been the first in those days to follow the party line like sheep.

Kreisky was another force of nature in the seventies.
Of course, Kreisky wasn't quite like Adolf.
There was no way the man on the street could get away from Kreisky.
I'm speaking here from experience.
At the time, I even had a stretch in the party.
It wasn't long before I got an apartment.
And my son got a job at the municipality just like me.
And it wasn't long before he got a cheap apartment as well.
Kreisky was a force of nature – at least in his early years.
But what came after Kreisky?
All I can say to that is: Good night Austria.
Karl says that the rabble clinging to Kreisky should've been chased out the country.
Then things would look very different today.
It was the same with Adolf.
Adolf was alright, but look at his followers.
Just the same as Kreisky.
These Kreiskyites handed out the jobs, the apartments and the money to each other.
Just as they needed it.
As soon as I realized what was going on I left the party.
I didn't want to have anything to do with it.
To be involved with people who just cherry pick what they wanted wasn't my thing.

I'm not that kind of guy.
It didn't take me long to realize what was going on.
It wasn't about honesty and ideals, it was about jobs, apartments and money.
That's why joining was a big mistake.
Karl said to me that he'd known the Red Falcons weren't the right people for me to mix with.
You get caught up and lost in the cogs of that big machine, he said.
Exactly, I said.

6

When whilst weeding those Russians and their police complaint shot into my head, I flew into a mad frenzy, hacking into those slugs with my trowel, again and again, until the slime was squirting everywhere.
I could suddenly see the whole mess so clearly.
And seeing those slugs' innards squishing all over made me feel a hell of a lot better.
Then I said to myself I shouldn't let those Russian bastards upset me.
There's no point.
As long as the government's full of Russians, nothing's going to change anyway.
So just forget it and tend your cabbages, I said to myself.
All the excitement will only give you a heart attack.
At fifty-five you're no longer a spring chicken.
It takes just seconds and then you're six feet under.
Popping your clogs just two years after retirement is much too early.
Those assholes would be delighted no doubt.
But that won't happen to Judge Georgie, no way.
Even if I do have a bad back, I'm certainly not going to bite the dust yet.
Just take care of your health, I tell myself, if you've got your health, you've got everything, I say.
Without it, you're lost.

That's not to say that other things aren't important like emotions, being humane, family, nature and all that.
Whenever I'm in the garden, I sense just how important nature is.
To me, nature means inner balance, well health I suppose.
The farther humankind distances itself from nature, the sicker it becomes.
I think the state should do something about it.
About nature.
I mean just think of the savings the state could make if it intervened.
If the state took better care of nature, paying for the diapers and incontinence pads of the poorest wouldn't be a problem.
It would resuscitate the health sector in one fell swoop.
After all, humans are nature and the state could save billions of dollars and all those chemicals if only people would stay close to nature.
But nature is of no value to the state.
Just in the same way as health isn't.
In fact, they're happy when you kick the bucket as soon as you retire because they save all that pension money.
That's how the state thinks.
That's why it's not interested in taking care of your health.
It suits them if you bite the dust.

7

I only really started enjoying my backyard when I retired.
Before then, I was only ever at home on the weekends.
I know my wife looked after it a little every now and then but she had enough to worry about, what with her aunt and her cleaning jobs.
She's a hardworking woman.
My second marriage was definitely a marriage of convenience.
I'm not afraid to admit it.
The way I see things now, a marriage is most likely to fail when you love someone.
If you love someone and then marry them, you're pretty much doomed.
Believe me, I know what I'm talking about.
I've seen it all with my own eyes.
You can't fool me, that's for sure.
But I also admit you're pretty stuck without a woman.
Especially back in the day when I was a traveling salesman.
Up country, down country, I got to see it all.
I've been all over.
You just don't have time to get things done when you're on the go all week.

Then you come home for the weekend and your apartment's cold and empty.

Last week's laundry's still strewn across the floor, the food-crusted crockery's still cluttering the worktop and the toilet seat's still full of pee...

That was my life after my divorce.

So, you can't tell me otherwise.

That's just the way it is.

It's nice when you come home and there's someone there waiting for you, it's warm, it's tidy and your dinner's on the table.

That's why I think family life's so important even though it may sound old-fashioned.

Well, I definitely learned from the first big mistake I made.

I didn't want to end up shit creek without a paddle again, that's for sure.

Once bitten and all that....

So when I got married for the second time we both signed a prenup.

That way everything was sorted on both sides.

Things have been good because it was a marriage of convenience.

She works hard, she's tidy, she's reliable, and even though she wasn't blessed with beauty, I'm more than happy with her.

She'd never been married before but had suffered some harsh disappointments.

She'd had some terrible relationships with men.
We all know what kind of men are on the loose out
there.
Destiny wasn't kind to her, that's for sure.
Your second wife is never like the first though.
First comes love, then comes prudence.
That's just the way it is.
Sad as it is.
It'd be better if prudence came first.
Believe me, I know what I'm talking about.
It would've saved me heaps of pain and disappoint-
ment if I'd known all that when I was younger.
But plenty of things are the wrong way round in life.
Pretty much everything really.

8

My divorce didn't just cost me the earth.
It took some getting over.
We were married for twelve years.
You can't just wipe away all those years at the drop
of a hat.
It's all dead and buried now though.
I have a few good memories left.
Especially from the early days before we got married.
I was a young good-looking guy, my God...
When I first met her I'd only just joined the Austrian
railroad.
Yeah, I was working for the Austrian railroad, be-
cause my father had worked there before me.
At the time, he got it all sorted through the party.
I was on the trains as a ticket inspector and she lived
on my route, not far from the station.
So I hopped off the train and ran off to her.
Not surprisingly, I wasn't a ticket inspector with the
ÖBB for much longer after that.
The Austrian railroad didn't have any sympathy for
that kind of love.
But then again, a ticket inspector's life wasn't for
me.
My father went crazy when he found out.
How can you give up a job in the civil service, blab-
labla....

But can you think of anything more tedious than being a ticket inspector?
It's always the same.
One station after the next.
The only thing that changes is the date on the ticket stamp.
Otherwise, it's always the same.
So, it's hardly surprising I always ran to her.
And anyway, I was head over heels in love with her.
Yes, I really was at the time.
I can say that hand on heart.
The two of us had many good times together.
Our first holidays camping in Italy were great.
We didn't have two cents to rub together, just enough to buy a pizza to share.
But it was still fantastic.
Even when the kids were young.
Jesolo, Riccione, Fano.
It was like a dream.
But life is what it is.
By that I mean that everything always ends so tragically.
There you are living together for years, thinking and believing everything's fine.
You think you've found someone you can grow old with and before you know it, it's all over.
Yep, before you know it.
Suddenly, your whole life's in tatters.

I guess I have Karl to thank for opening my eyes.
Hey George, he once said to me after a soccer match, just keep an eye on that wife of yours, ok?
He said it in a tone that was quite unlike him.
Karl's the funniest guy you can imagine.
He always has a joke up his sleeve, always full of shenanigans.
My problem is that I'm far too trusting.
At the time, I was away all week and only home on the weekend.
Of course, we had our issues from time to time.
Anyone who says they never have problems is lying through their teeth.
When Karl said that to me, I knew she was playing away.
That was as clear as day.
I raced home like a mad man.
First of all, she denied everything, but then she gradually came out with the truth...
So that was all the thanks I got for working my fingers to the bone for my family.
She said we'd drifted apart, I didn't give her enough attention when I was home, I didn't make an effort, she said she felt like the cleaner and wasn't prepared to be exploited or chained to the home any longer.
The only thing you leave behind when you go are your dirty socks and a filthy toilet seat, etcetera...
It was all my fault, of course.

It was a stab in the heart when she broke our trust like that.

A man does have his pride, you know.

OK, I may have had a few little flings along the way myself.

But when you're on the road all week, sacrificing yourself for your family, you need a little human warmth.

I'm not a monk after all said and done.

And it was all quite harmless anyway.

I guess I just saved on motel costs which helped the family as well because it meant I was bringing more money home.

But then, gratitude is a rare commodity in this life.

It was alright for her.

There she was at home, quite the lady of leisure, with her own car and all – I was earning big bucks back then, you see.

It's not as though the money was pouring in, of course; I had to work hard for it.

I never bought anything for myself.

Sometimes, I'd go with Karl to the match, or sometimes we'd get smashed every now and then.

But that was it.

I never even worked in the backyard because I just didn't have time.

She wasn't interested in that kind of thing anyway.

I'll get those cabbages and beans at the grocery store, a backyard is just a pain in the butt, she'd say.

There's no point.
Not surprisingly, she bought all those cabbages and vegetables with my hard-earned cash.
She sure took that for granted.
She didn't have the time of day for anything to do with nature.
She took it for granted in the same way she took for granted all the money I brought home every month.
People who have no time for nature have no time for people either.
That's what I've learned in life.
That's the truth.
If I'd know then what I know now, none of this would ever have happened.
I know what I'm talking about these days.
No-one can pull the wool over my eyes anymore.

9

Those were tough times back then.
For me, at least.
To top it all, it was a traveling salesman just like me, who was saving motel costs by sleeping with my ex-wife and she even believed she'd found the love of her life.
Only women can be so naive.
Once I heard someone say you can get bed and breakfast for free from Judge Georgie's wife.
Imagine how humiliated I felt.
I couldn't believe it was happening to me.
I raced home down the freeway at 125m/h.
I'm the kind of man who likes clear-cut situations.
When I confronted her, her jaw dropped and her teeth shattered.
It was a set of false ones from the health insurance.
We could've gone our separate ways like two sensible adults.
But no, that doesn't seem possible in Austria.
It was she who wanted the divorce.
She had to after playing away like that.
And then there were her good friends who filled her head with magic.
Once a woman has made up her mind about something there's simply no cure for it.
Once again, Karl hit the nail on the head.

You have one big flaw, he said: You were always much too nice to her.

She had too much time on her hands and she was treated too well.

Just like our soccer players who want to feather their nests without coming up with the goods.

But that only works for so long.

After a match once – it must've been way past midnight – Karl said to me, you should put your wife on the transfer list because she's already playing for another team.

And that's just the way it was.

When women have too much time on their hands, they come up with all sorts of ideas, Karl said.

God only knows how right he was.

To top it all, her friends persuaded her that her discontent was real.

When it comes to the crunch, a divorce is like a car wreck. You never get through it without shouldering some of the blame.

That's just the way the Austrian courts work.

In Austria the victims are treated like criminals.

That was the case with my divorce anyway.

Her lawyer wanted to pile all the blame on me; they accused me of mental cruelty. They said a few well-earned slaps made me a wife batterer. And they wasted no time mentioning the false teeth without going into any of the detail.

Yes, we're all too familiar with that.

They stoop real low to get their own way.

Of course she got a slap or two.

Was I supposed to stand on the sidelines while she was having fun between the sheets with someone else?

Especially with some salesman from the competition.

It wasn't long before we were the talk of the town and you can imagine what my colleagues all thought of me.

That's all in the past now, best forgotten.

She portrayed me as a domineering bully and monster who treated his wife like dirt.

In court, I asked her how that was possible if I was never at home anyway.

The fact that she'd thrown a vase at me was quite acceptable, of course, because the poor woman was so suppressed and helpless.

It was pure self defense, the lawyer had said.

Being the respectable citizen I am, I would never have imagined what goes on in Austrian courts.

One thing's for sure, the Austrian courts are the pits; they're the worst.

Possibly in the world.

Sadly, I didn't realize what a false bitch my ex-wife was until it was too late.

So from that point of view, we should've got divorced much sooner.

If there's one thing I can't stand, it's phony people.
I'd say it's on a par with justice.
In my eyes, these things simply aren't up for debate.
When she moved out, she even tried to get her claws on my car, because I'd taken hers away from her – quite understandably, I think.
I was going to tamper with it so she'd smash into a tree or an embankment.
But then I decided it was a bad idea.
I was scared they'd find out and then I'd be up shit creek again.
But I couldn't believe her cheek with my car. It was crazy!
One of her friends went and stood in the way.
I ran over as fast as I could, pushing her over, grabbing and pulling my ex-wife out of the car, just as she was starting the engine.
Her friend was sprawled out on the ground.
Shrieking for help.
I gave my wife a good clout.... we were practically already divorced.
Down at the police station... well, you know how easily the truth is twisted.
The two women were bosom buddies.
Going by their version of events, I only just stopped short of killing them.
There's nothing as insincere as women.
OK, maybe they're not all like that but...

It's easy to twist the truth though, right?!
While my car's being stolen, a hulk of a woman
blocks my way and then has the audacity to stand
up in court and demand compensation.
But then, that's Austria for you.

10

I was in a really dark place back then.
I was pushed to my absolute limits.
If it had gone on for much longer, God only knows...
I toyed with the idea on more than one occasion of driving up to the Europa Bridge and jumping off it.
Things like that were constantly going through my mind.
At the same time though, I also learned the value of friends.
If I hadn't had Karl, I don't know what I'd have done.
He gave me so much comfort.
That bitch isn't worth crying over, he'd say.
I'll never forget how he stood by me at that difficult time.
Now, looking back, I don't really care anymore.
My ex-wife definitely wasn't worth jumping off the Europa Bridge over.
It would've been better if she'd ploughed into a tree because her brakes had failed.
You only think such crazy thoughts in situations like that.
The bad thing about a divorce is always the kids.
Picking them up for the weekend once a fortnight and delivering them back on the Sunday night like a package at the post office.

Those were the saddest Sundays of my life.
I'm pretty tough in many ways, but it would break my heart when the three of us would sit at a diner on a Sunday afternoon, the kids polishing off one ice cream after the next.
My ex-wife didn't want me to see the kids at all, because she said their school work always suffered when they'd been with me for the weekend.
Only women can hate so blindly.
A man hasn't the capacity to hate like a woman.
Believe me, it's true.
If I didn't know what I was talking about, I'd keep my mouth shut.
I can just picture how my ex-wife would rave on and on after the kids had visited me.
I wanted to spare the children all the fuss.
In spite of everything, they all grew into decent human beings though.
Of course, they got most of their good traits from me, especially when it comes to being hard-working and sincere.
Qualities that are fairly rare these days.
Just look around you.

11

Karl never really liked my wife.
He never said so, not until after the divorce.
You can find another one like her on every street cor-
ner, he'd said.
But even so.
I know what a man goes through during a divorce.
You can't fool me.
I experienced it first hand.
It's all in the past now.
I never really think about it anymore.
Why should I?
There's no point in continuing a marriage when the
trust between you has been destroyed.
The only way is to call it quits.
My ex-wife and I completely lost sight of each oth-
er.
I guess.
She married again.
Not very happily, or so I've heard.
But there you go.
Everyone gets their just reward.
Why should she be alright?
I don't want her to be well.
Healthwise.
Some bad illness.
Hmmm.

If we were still married, then I'd have that to deal with as well.

So, sometimes life does make sense after all.

12

When I told Karl about my latest plan, he nearly toppled off his chair laughing.
First he thought I was joking when I told him about the moat I wanted round my backyard.
Then at least, I'd block out all those disgusting slugs from the neighbors'.
They'd all drown before they even got a sniff at my backyard.
All I'd have to do is dig and concrete a small channel all around the edge and then I'd be rid of those slimy slugs; stamping out those critters is child's play.
But all these slugs and snails come from far and wide.
I guess they know where to find the best meals in town.
I can kill off my own slugs without a problem.
Hmm, nature didn't mean a thing to my first wife.
But why in hell am I thinking of her again?
I struck that bitch from my memory long ago.
I don't go to Church, but there they say: We are of dust and return to dust.
You can rephrase it to: We are of nature and return to nature.
Being so attached to my backyard probably has something to do with my childhood.
My mother always had a large backyard, with potatoes and all.

If we hadn't had the backyard, we would've starved after the War.
My mother often used to say this.
Five children and a father working on the railroads; times weren't rosy then.
But it soon got better.
Trained as a bricklayer, my dad put up one house after another after work.
They were known as the railroad crew.
The thing is, you see, you get plenty of free time working for the railroad.
But if he hadn't worked so hard, we wouldn't have survived.
Not with five kids and a salary from the railroad.
But my parents were hard-working people.
My father paid for it in the end though.
One morning, he just didn't wake up. Fifty-three, he was.
He'd had a heart attack in his sleep.
It must've been a nice way to go.
But not at his age.
He didn't get to enjoy any of his retirement.
He'd worked himself to death.
All for the sake of his family.
That's the way people were in the old days.
If he hadn't worked for the railroad, he would've popped his clogs much sooner.
His job on the railroad was a walk in the park.

He did a lot of night shifts.
And during the day, he worked on the construction sites.
Over time, it really took its toll.
Going for years more or less without sleep, and then one day, when the worst is over, he doesn't wake up.
Fate has no mercy on anyone or anything.
My father was more than strict with us.
But we respected him.
One word was all it took and we obeyed.
The same was true of Mom.
There was no messing with them.
And that's the truth.
But he was fair and just.
My Mom always said that, out of all us kids, I was most like him.
My Dad was a simple man.
I still think of him often.
He was a good man and always stayed on the straight and narrow.
At least when he closed his eyes for the final time, he could rest with a clear conscience.
This has been my lifelong goal as well.
Always to keep face, to keep up appearances.
When my number's up, I want to rest with a clear conscience.
That's what's important in life.

Karl always says there are enough assholes in this world and that very few people can actually walk tall.
That's just the way it is.

13

Last week I was at the trade show in Salzburg.
Sometimes when my boss needs me, I help him out.
Especially at trade shows and events like that.
You need to have a feel for it, you see.
You've either got it or you ain't.
A salesman's got to have it; if he doesn't, he might as well pack up and go home.
I don't want to blow my own trumpet but my boss always says to me: A guy like Judge Georgie is one of a kind.
My boss always appreciated me.
We were like friends.
If I hadn't had him after the divorce, I'd be on the streets today, the way she tried to take me to the cleaners.
But my boss has been there too – once bitten, and all that.
Three divorces, he's had.
He said to me, George, I'll do anything to help you out.
I'd have paid through the nose, if it hadn't been for him.
Luckily, he paid me a lot of my wages in cash, so my ex wouldn't get her sticky fingers on my money.
She tried everything.
But she was banging her head against a brick wall when it came to us.

I know loads of men who've lost a fortune getting divorced.

Some are so broke, they haven't got two cents to rub together.

Frau Dohnal, the minister for women and proverbial vampire, did a good job of it.

She was only loved by the women because she attracted the frustrated souls of this earth.

And the majority of women are frustrated.

You can forget them all.

That's the truth.

I know what I'm talking about.

You can't pull the wool over my eyes.

I've seen and experienced far too much.

They expect you to be on your knees day and night, and even then it's never enough.

When I think of all the things my ex-wife demanded.

But I left her nothing, except for our home.

Even so, I got off lightly.

Based on my salary, I would've been bled dry.

But thankfully my boss was on my side.

That's why I'm happy to help him when he calls.

And besides, it's a bit of extra cash in my pocket.

As a pensioner, every euro counts.

I had a field day last time I was in Salzburg.

I always enjoyed going to the trade shows in Salzburg.

Whenever I go to a trade show I stay at the hotel "Himmelreich".

That's the way it's always been.
The "Himmelreich" is where all the other salesmen go as well because it's still such good value for money.
That doesn't mean it's cheap, by God no, but we salesmen get a special rate, you see.
The concierge alone is worth his weight in gold.
He's already part of the inventory.
He knows the best chicks in Salzburg and turns a blind eye when you take one of them to your room.
He's as silent as a grave.
In the evenings, a live eight-man band plays at the hotel.
Where else can you find that these days?
Of course, I didn't hear the band last week because these trade shows really take it out of you.
Never to bed and gallons of liquor...
But the next day, you have to be on top form and give one hundred and fifty percent.
That's trade shows for you.
My face looked like it'd been hit by a bus.
This week I didn't get much more than ten hours sleep.
It'd be tough getting through it without medication and eye drops.
These trade shows really get to you and they really do my back in.
Sometimes I can barely stand up straight.
But then you just have to grit your teeth and carry on.

And it seems to get harder every year.
My boss is already thinking of selling up, even though the company's going well.
Business was definitely easier in the past.
The money just kept on rolling in.
Today, the competition seems to be creaming it all off, even though the packaging industry's still growing.
We specialize solely in packaging.
Especially plastics.
Today, pretty much everything is packaged.
Even the corpses in the morgues are wrapped in our films.
But the boss is still thinking of selling up.
Sooner or later, he says, I'll be swallowed by one of the big players.
I might as well enjoy a few years of freedom, he says.
He's currently negotiating with a German company.
So, we might be in Salzburg for the final time this year, the boss laughed.
I got the feeling he said it mainly in jest though.
Be that as it may, this week was damn tough.
It really takes it out of you.
And what with my wife being in hospital.
I couldn't even visit her.
Hysterectomy.
Broken machinery.
There's nothing more to say about it really.

And there's nothing to be done about it either.
It's all got a bit much for her lately.
First, the carry on with the Russians and the relatives, especially that shady stepson.
Then her aunt's death.
That really upset her.
Even though it was the best thing for her aunt.
This life had nothing more to offer her.
The poor woman had suffered enough.
She was away with the fairies for the majority of the time.
Completely lost and out of it.
It's all behind her now.
But it was a real burden on my wife.
That's why she's in such a bad way.
It's mostly psychological with her.
I'm actually quite glad I didn't have to go to the hospital.
When that smell shoots up my nostrils, I have to get out fast.
Wherever possible I avoid visiting people in hospital.
Thanks to Salzburg I didn't have to go.
It was out of my hands.
She's coming home tomorrow.
I've been speaking to her on the phone every day.
She's also got a TV in her room.
Even a video.
I can't go and see her today.

Not in the state I'm in, I didn't get to bed till four in the morning again.

It's madness, but quite normal.

It was like an encore to Salzburg.

What with the car and the waitress from the Mona Lisa.

If they took away my driver's license today, I'd still get by, I guess.

But in the past, it would've been a disaster.

They caught me three times.

Once, I got three months.

Being on the road for three months without a license, is more than just risky.

But what was I supposed to do.

The wife and the kids had to be fed.

None of them cares whether or not you have a license...

Thank God I didn't get caught.

I mustn't forget to go to the travel agent's today.

Because of Karl's birthday present.

He won't believe his eyes when he gets his gift.

The flight and the week; it'll cost a packet.

But I'm more than happy to splash out on Karl like that.

And anyway, all five of us are clubbing together.

Everyone likes Karl.

With five chipping in, we'll be spreading out the cost nicely.

Epilog

Right, that's it!
There comes a time in all situations where enough is enough.
Even though it's really got nothing to do with me.
Well, I wouldn't say it has nothing to do with me, because I get upset when my wife is upset even though I did warn her right from the start.
I got a lawyer on the case right away.
I don't care about the costs, even if eats away at all the savings books.
We'll show this pathetic excuse for a stepson, if he thinks he can defame my wife like that.
We have a lawsuit pending against him for defamation with claims for compensation as well.
After all, we are someone and we won't be dragged through the dirt by some pathetic loser.
I don't have time for that.
The stepson's contesting the will because of the house and the savings books that have apparently mysteriously disappeared.
He's got a neck on him, unbelievable.
This leach has been sponging off others all his life and then has the audacity to make demands.
At any rate, if there's any justice in this world…

But then we live in Austria...
In Austria we've got to the point where the freeload-
ers have the say.
The Russian mafia and the boot necks make the
rules round here now.
It breaks my heart to see things go downhill so fast
in Austria.
Somehow, I'm kind of attached to this country.
After all, I did my bit to help build it.
Even if I was just a small cog in a big wheel.
Things were always on the up and up.
Back in the day.
But wealth hasn't done the majority of people any
good at all.
Prosperity has ruined this country.
The Russians and spongers are spreading.
As each day goes by.
Just like in my vegetable patch.
And instead of nipping it in the bud, these pilfering
scumbags are getting support from up there.
Hard-working, law-abiding citizens are the fools
these days.
Just like my wife.
But I did warn her.
If you're good, you're stupid.
No-one took care of her aunt when she was poorly.
But now there's money up for grabs, he's right at the
front of the line, Mr Almighty Stepson.

Her aunt must be turning in her grave.
Thank God, she's not here to witness it.
She knew what she was doing when she wrote her Will the way she did.
She was all too aware it would be wasted on rounds of drinks, if she didn't re-write it.
We've got to put a stop to these cheats, Karl said.
But who, I ask, is going to do stand up and do it?
Certainly not the waffling politicians who are ruling our country.
The only thing they're good at is squeezing the small, hard-working man on the street.
Yes, taking away their incontinence pads and diapers.
Sometimes, I'm really not surprised people plant bombs.
If you're cajoled and battered for long enough, what other options are you left with?
You're forced into doing it – it's self-defense.
It's a wonder that not more bombs go off.
There's no other way of defending yourself, because we're in Austria.
These Russians and freeloaders can only be controlled by taking radical measures.
The country needs to be ruled with a rod of iron.
A real act of nature is what it needs
Without a force of nature, it'll be impossible to get the country back in shape.

The only hope for someone like me is an act of God.
Without it, this country has no future.
This Austria.
On your own, you've got no chance against the mafia.
Your life's work ruined.
I know what I'm talking about.
If I didn't know better, I'd keep my mouth shut.
Nothing else will fix it.
The only way is a radical act of God.
I've seen and experienced enough.
No-one can pull the wool over my eyes anymore.

About „Austria.Karl"
from InTranslation, Brooklyn Rail Sept. 2014

Author Elias Schneitter masters quite supremely the dramatic art of portraying the overlooked and the apparently petty and trivial. This is particularly true of Schneitter's anthology of short narratives entitled Austria. Karl. The story chosen for InTranslation is all about "Judge Georgie" who in a very revealing monolog points the accusatory finger at the world, complaining about everything in general and Austria (otherwise referred to in Austria as Karl), foreigners, the government and the snails in his garden in particular. He is certainly not a judge by profession but is a notorious grumbler, who never minces his words and freely gives vent to his many blind prejudices. He always blames others for the unfortunate twists and turns his life has taken, never questioning his own decisions or views. The story of Judge Georgie is one of self-deception and self-justification. It is just one of several internal monologs that make up this anthology that also features Ernst who reflects on his former career on a cruise liner and Walter, the hippy in the military uniform. Elias Schneitter is very much interested in the "man on the street" and the contradictions that define them. He describes his characters with laconic wit, but always treats them with respect and empathy.

Isabelle Esser

Elias Schneitter

was born and grew up in
Zirl in Tyrol, Austria. After
completing his schooling in
Stams, he had a variety of
jobs, working in souvenirs,
as an office clerk, a canoeing teacher in Sturgeon Lake
- Minnesota, a project manager for Ho-Ruck, a social
program for former inmates, and as an employee for
the Austrian social security system. Today, he works as
a freelance author. He is co-founder of the international
literature festival "sprachsalz" in Hall, Tyrol and head of
the small publishing house "edition-baes".

His first publications started appearing from 1974,
mainly in literary magazines (Fenster, Rampe, wespenest,
protokolle, projektil) and as radio plays. His first book
was published in 1979 (geflügelte worte). In 2014, he
was presented with the Kathy Acker Award for his com-
mitment to promoting international literature, above all,
between the USA and the German-speaking world.

www.edition-baes.com